Sir Gadabout
Out of Time

Other brilliant *Sir Gadabout* books
by Martyn Beardsley

Sir Gadabout
Sir Gadabout Gets Worse
Sir Gadabout and the Ghost
Sir Gadabout Goes Barking Mad
Sir Gadabout Does His Best
Sir Gadabout and the Little Horror
Sir Gadabout Goes Overboard
Sir Gadabout Goes to Knight School

You can find out more about Sir Gadabout at
http://martian57.googlepages.com/home

Martyn Beardsley

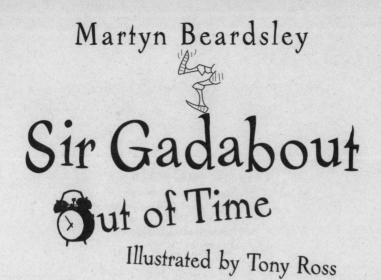

Sir Gadabout
Out of Time

Illustrated by Tony Ross

Orion
Children's Books

First published in Great Britain in 2007
by Orion Children's Books
a division of the Orion Publishing Group Ltd
Orion House
5 Upper St Martin's Lane
London WC2H 9EA
An Hachette Livre UK Company

1 3 5 7 9 10 8 6 4 2

The Orion Publishing Group's policy is to use papers that
are natural, renewable and recyclable products and made
from wood grown in sustainable forests. The logging and
manufacturing processes are expected to conform to the
environmental regulations of the country of origin.

Printed in Great Britain by Clays Ltd, St Ives plc

ISBN 978 1 84255 615 3

www.orionbooks.co.uk

Contents

1

Just a Snip Here and There

A long, long time ago – even before that new *Blue Peter* presenter joined the programme (I preferred the old ones myself) – there lived a famous barber called Simeon Snippett. He was so good at hairdressing that pop stars, actors and people who had been on *Big Brother* came from miles around to have their hair done by him. He could even cut the hair of knights while they still had their helmets on – which is partly how he got his latest job.

His fame reached the ears of the famous and much-loved King Arthur. His Majesty ruled from within the mighty walls of Camelot, a castle hidden far away in mists and dark forests, where owls hooted, wolves howled, and few people dared to tread. (Except on Sundays and bank holidays, when Camelot held open days with bouncy castles, ice-cream vans, and a very good gift shop selling Knights of the Round Table tea-towels and Lady of the Lake lavender bath salts.)

King Arthur had rather thick, frizzy hair that seemed to have a mind of its own. The beautiful Queen Guinevere usually cut it, and made a pretty good job of it. She could turn her hand to most things: if ever you attend a Camelot open day, have a look at the *CamelotzKool* baseball caps in the gift shop. She ran them up in an afternoon on her sewing machine. *And* she'd made the sewing machine!

Simeon Snippet came to be the Royal Barber when King Arthur's hair was getting too long and sticking up all over the place, and Queen Guinevere was at her mum's for a few days landscaping her garden. Snippet was invited to cut the royal hair, and King Arthur was so impressed that he was chosen to be the Royal Barber in Residence.

But then another day came when King Arthur's hair was getting too long, and Queen Guinevere was helping NASA out with a problem on their *Mars Probe Seven*. *And*, as luck would have it, Simeon Snippet had gone along to hold the spanners for her (and for a bit of a holiday, it must be admitted).

King Arthur was looking at his hair in a mirror and trying to flatten the sticky-out

bits, when he saw a knight walking by. Now, although he liked the way both Guinevere and Simeon Snippet cut his hair, the king didn't really think that snipping a few bits of hair could be particularly hard. In fact, he thought that anyone could do it. And when he saw this knight walking by, he had a brainwave . . .

If Queen Guinevere had been there, she might have said that if he was going to let a knight cut his hair, it might just be better not to choose this one. But then, Queen Guinevere liked this particular knight, so she wouldn't say anything *too* bad about him. If anyone else had been there, they might have warned the king that if he let *this* knight loose on him with a pair of scissors, he was likely to die a bloody and bizarre death before the job was done. For this particular Knight was Sir Gadabout, known by all as the Worst Knight in the World.

Sir Gadabout had just got back from a mission to slay a troublesome dragon in the wealthy kingdom of Belgravia. While there,

he managed to blow up
the Prince Regent's
bicycle, drop the
Crown Jewels down
a toilet, and ended up
chasing the dragon
with the Queen of
Belgravia's mother-in-law

in its mouth all the way across the
Himalayas.

But just because Sir Gadabout single-
handedly turned the Kingdom of Belgravia
into a devastated, smoking ruin (you might
have seen the moving documentary they
showed about it all on the Belgravia

Discovery Channel,
*How Could it Come
to This?*), it doesn't
mean to say that he
couldn't cut hair.
And King Arthur,
who had personally
visited the Prince
Regent of Belgravia in

5

hospital (he had been on his bike at the time) and taken him a box of chocolates, thought that some of the stories about Sir Gadabout were exaggerated. They just *had* to be. So he sat in the chair and let the Worst Knight in the World have a go at his hair.

Sir Gadabout was ably assisted by his loyal squire Herbert. Herbert was a short but powerfully built youth who would never hear a bad word said about his master. During the hair-cutting, he stood nearby ready to hand over the scissors, mallet, and other implements Sir Gadabout thought he might need.

"Just a snip there, and a few here . . ." mumbled Sir Gadabout as he busied himself with the scissors. He was soon enjoying it so much that he began to wonder about taking this up full-time.

"I was wondering," gasped King Arthur, "if you really needed to twist my head round so much?"

"You've got a wonderfully flexible neck,

Your Majesty!" Sir Gadabout said admiringly. "Your head nearly goes all the way round!"

"But I'm not sure it's supposed to—" squeaked the King.

"You could walk round and do his fringe from the front, sire," Herbert suggested quietly.

"I never thought of that! There's more to this hair-cutting business than meets the eye!"

King Arthur felt sure that the pile of hair on the floor was never quite so big when Simeon did it . . .

"Now, this is a tough bit," said Sir Gadabout. "Pass me the Big Scissors, if you please, Herbert."

"Here you are, sire."

"Hmm, still not right. Pass me the Bigger Scissors."

"Er, those look like hedge shears," said King Arthur worriedly.

"Yes, they would," said Sir Gadabout, lost in a little hairdressing world of his own.

"Now, *this* bit's even trickier. Have we got a saw or something, Herbert?"

"NO!" cried the King.

"Quite right, Your Majesty," agreed Herbert. "We haven't got one of those."

"Oh well. Just have to put Plan B into action."

"Oww!" cried the King. "I much preferred Plan A."

"We can soon put a sticking-plaster on that," Sir Gadabout cheerfully reassured him.

Finally, it was done.

"Before we show His Majesty the mirror, what do you think?" Sir Gadabout asked Herbert.

"Very good for a beginner, sire. I'd say the left side is a mite better than the right, but you'd hardly notice in the dark. Perhaps you should have taken his crown off before you started."

Sir Gadabout passed the mirror to King Arthur. At first, the King held the mirror in front of his face with his eyes tightly shut. Then he slowly, as if by a great effort, peeled one eye open. Then he shut it tightly again as if he didn't want to see any more, and he began to breathe so hard and fast that bubbles came out of his nose. It was several minutes before he could bring himself to open both eyes.

"I can see that Your Majesty is excited." Sir Gadabout smiled. "Just think what I could do with a bit of practise!"

King Arthur *was* thinking. He was thinking that his hair looked as though it had been savaged by a mad dog. He was thinking that there were places where tufts of hair stuck up like carrot tops, and shiny white patches where there was no hair at all. He was thinking that he looked like the picture of the Ghoul from the Graveyard in a book which had given him nightmares as a child. But he was a very nice man, and he hated hurting Sir Gadabout's feelings.

"It's very . . . *different*. The problem is, I've got an important meeting with the Queen of Poland tomorrow, and I'm worried that she might be afraid – er, I mean, afraid that it's not really me. Because I look so interestingly different."

"Are you *sure* you like it, Your Majesty?" Sir Gadabout asked.

"Oh, yes, Gads. It's just that the Queen of Poland hasn't seen me in a long time and she might be terrified – I mean, terrified that I've been kidnapped and replaced by another person or something . . ."

Sir Gadabout shrugged. "Oh well, I'll just have another go at it. We hairdressers are good at sorting things out when—"

"*No!*" cried the king. "Er, I've taken up too much of your time already. What I was thinking was that we could get Merlin to use a spell to sort it out."

"Well," said Sir Gadabout, picking up the Bigger Scissor, "it would only take a minute to—"

"*Merlin!*" repeated the king, nervously. "Would you go and get him? Now? Please?"

Sir Gadabout reluctantly put the Bigger Scissors down. "Right away, Your Majesty."

2

Bombs Away!

The great wizard Merlin lived in a cottage a short distance from Camelot. To get there you had to follow a narrow path deep into the Willow Woods; it was dark and cool even on the sunniest day, and the ancient, overgrown path was easy to lose sight of. There was always a feeling that someone was watching you from the dark shadows amongst the trees and thickly-growing bushes.

Sir Gadabout had been known to find it all too much and run back out screaming before even reaching Merlin's cottage. But that was when he was on his own. When he was with someone else, he was much braver.

And as if finding the cottage wasn't enough, once you found it, another challenge lay ahead . . .

Sir Gadabout pushed open the rickety gate at the bottom of Merlin's garden, and he and Herbert ventured in. They did so rather cautiously, because on previous visits some very strange things had happened at about this time.

Halfway down the garden path, a post in the ground with a sign nailed to it blocked their progress. Scrawled on it in green paint were the words THIS WAY and an arrow pointing towards Merlin's lawn. Sir Gadabout and Herbert dutifully followed the arrow, and they came to a large white cross marked in the middle of the lawn. Right in the centre of the cross was another sign hammered into the ground. This one said, WAIT HERE!

"This is very strange, I must say, sire."

"Better do as the sign says," said Sir Gadabout. "I always believe in—"

"What was that funny noise, sire?"

interrupted Herbert, looking all around him.

"I can't hear any . . . wait a minute . . . yes – it's a kind of buzzing noise . . ."

They both looked up, down and all around, but couldn't make out where the sound was coming from. It sounded like an angry swarm of bees.

Then, suddenly, a dark shape swooped into view above them. It was Dr McPherson, Merlin's guard-turtle, in a model aeroplane, zooming low over their heads. When he was right above them, he cried, "BOMBS AWAY!" and a large door opened up in the

15

bottom of his plane. A bomb dropped out –
but too soon. Instead of heading for Sir
Gadabout and Herbert, it was falling towards
Merlin's cottage. Then Dr McPherson, who
hadn't seen his mistake, attempted to do a
victorious loop-the-loop in his plane. It shot
upwards, but as it did so he tumbled back
and fell through the open bomb-door.

"*Yaaaaargh!*" cried Dr McPherson.

The bomb plummeted straight down
Merlin's chimney.

Seconds later, Dr McPherson followed it.

There was a muffled BOOM, and Dr
McPherson came streaking back out of the
chimney like a rocket on bonfire night.

"*Waaaaaaaaaaaah!*" He soared into the sky
till he was a tiny speck.

Seconds later, the cottage door flew open.
A cloud of black smoke billowed out, and
in the middle of it stumbled the wizard
Merlin and Sidney Smith, his rather moody
ginger cat. They were as black as the smoke,
coughing and spluttering, frazzled, and *very*
angry.

"I suppose it makes a change from pressing
a doorbell," commented Sir Gadabout.

"Yes," agreed Herbert. "But you wouldn't
want too many visitors in one day."

They helped Merlin and Sidney Smith to
clean up the cottage — which didn't take
long, since Merlin quite *liked* it to be dusty
and untidy. There was a large suitcase by
the front door, and once it was time for Sir
Gadabout to tell Merlin why he had come,
the wizard said, "I'm afraid you'll have to

17

make it quick – I was just about to leave for the annual Wizards' Convention in Blackpool."

When Sir Gadabout quickly tried to explain how he had cut King Arthur's hair and how it hadn't turned out *quite* the way the king wanted it, cat-like tittering could be heard coming from under the table. This was Sidney Smith, who knew just what Sir Gadabout was like and could well imagine what state the King's hair was in by now.

"If you don't stop your sniggering, you flea-bitten moggy," warned Herbert while Sir Gadabout taught Merlin the finer points of hairdressing, "I'll come under there and pull your whiskers out one by one!"

"Ha!" scoffed the cat. "I'll get my master to turn you into a thick lump of wood. Oh, I was forgetting – you already are one!"

"Why, you—," growled Herbert, about to dive under the table.

"Now, now," said Merlin sternly. He was tall and thin, and in his great dark cloak with silver moons and stars on it he had an air of mysterious powerfulness about him. "We must find a way to sort out the king's hair before he meets the Queen of Poland. I just haven't got time to go to Camelot."

He scratched his long, grey, straggly hair (Sir Gadabout was thinking of the things he could do with *that*), and thought for a moment, then went over to an old bookcase packed with large, dusty, leather-bound volumes.

"I've got it!" he said, pulling a dark red book from a shelf and blowing the dust from it. "In here is a simple Turning Back Time spell." He handed the book to Sir Gadabout. "Anyone can do it."

There was more cat-like chortling from under the table. "Anyone except *him*!"

"It's Spell 27 on page 74, near the back of the book," Merlin explained to Sir Gadabout, ignoring the cat.

"Got it," said Sir Gadabout. "It's in Book 74, near the back of page 27, and, er . . ."

"*Ha!*" said the cat-like voice under the table.

"Let me write it down for you," sighed

Merlin, snatching up a piece of paper and his quill pen. After quickly scribbling the instructions, he folded the note up and gave it to Sir Gadabout. "Now, I really must be on my way. But don't worry – I'm sending Sidney Smith with you to make sure things go all right."

"*Awww!*" groaned a cat-like voice.

And so, Sir Gadabout, Herbert and Sidney Smith set off for Camelot. Herbert had the spell book tucked safely under his stout arm. Sir Gadabout was convinced he didn't need the note; he was holding it still folded in his hand and trying to remember the instructions while they walked.

"It's near the back of spell 72, in the book at the end of . . ."

As they were walking past O'Blimey's Pond, there was a peculiar whistling noise. It got louder and louder, and closer and closer. They all looked up just in time to see Dr McPherson falling from the sky at an alarming rate of knots.

"Yeeeeeeeeeeeeaaaaaaaaaargh!"

He landed slap in the middle of O'Blimey's Pond. A gigantic fountain of water erupted into the air sending Sir Gadabout, Herbert and Sidney Smith scattering. Cats hate water, and Sidney Smith shot up a very tall tree. Herbert landed in a bed of stinging nettles. Sir Gadabout unfortunately scattered the wrong way, and fell in the pond after Dr McPherson.

When things had settled down, Sidney Smith crept cautiously back down to the ground and tip-toed through the puddles. Herbert came hopping out of the nettles doing a funny little dance: *"Oooh! Aah! Ouch! Eek!"*

Sir Gadabout waded out of the water. "I saved Merlin's instructions!" he exclaimed, holding the piece of paper aloft.

"Oh yeah?" said Sidney Smith. "What does it say, then?"

Sir Gadabout proceeded to unfold the note. Or tried to. The sodden paper fell to pieces in his hands, and the writing on what was left was just a shapeless blur of black ink, like one of those things that wins modern art prizes.

"Hmmm," said Sir Gadabout. "Anyway, I can remember it. It's the 77th spell at the back of the book . . . no, *near* the back of the book, on page 77, spell 24 . . . or is it . . ."

"*Heeelp!*" cried the distant voice of Dr McPherson, floating serenely on his back in O'Blimey's Pond as Sir Gadabout, Herbert and Sidney Smith headed off once more for Camelot.

The Time Spell

Back at Camelot, King Arthur was gazing wistfully into the mirror. He had tried hair gel, glue, goose fat, sticky tape and the bits of hair from the floor, and even boot polish to cover up the bare white patches, but nothing seemed to work.

He tried a variety of hats. There was a nice red and white woolly one which Guinevere had knitted him — but it was the middle of summer and much too hot for that. Then there was the green one which Sir Gadabout had knitted him. Amazingly, Sir Gadabout had followed the knitting pattern perfectly. Unfortunately, the pattern had been for a

teddy bear's cardigan, not a hat, and it somehow didn't look quite right on his head.

Then a servant came in and announced
the arrival of Sir Gadabout, and King Arthur's
spirits rose. Well, just a little.

"We have the solution, Your Majesty!" said
Sir Gadabout, waving the dark-red leather
volume in the air. "Merlin has given us a
simple spell – anyone can do it."

"*Tee-hee!*" said Sidney Smith.

But King Arthur sighed with relief, and
watched as Sir Gadabout leafed through the
thick book. And watched. And watched.

"Er, you do know which spell it is?" the
King queried. "It's just that there seem to be
an awful lot of them in there . . ."

"Oh, yes, Your Majesty. Won't be a
jiffy . . ."

"He'll turn the king *into* a jiffy!" chuckled
Sidney Smith quietly. Herbert tweaked his
tail.

"Now then," said Sir Gadabout, licking
his finger and turning the pages. "Spell 47,
but near spell 74, at the back . . . must be here

somewhere . . . Ah-HA! Spell 74, page 27. Time-altering Spell! Got it!"

"Thank goodness!" said King Arthur.

"Right," said Sir Gadabout. "If Your Majesty would stand perfectly still while I say the words, I shall make you just as you were before I cut your hair."

"Righto," agreed the King eagerly.

Sir Gadabout hesitated. "Are you really sure you want to do this? I mean, your new hair-do is beginning to grow on me – especially that bit on the left that looks like a little bunny. It's cute!"

"I thought it looked more like a giraffe and a poodle having a fight," mused Herbert.

"But that's the good thing about it," Sir Gadabout enthused. "You see something different every time you study it!"

King Arthur shuddered. "Just do the spell, if you please, Gads."

"Oh, well!" He read the words in the book carefully, then began to chant in the King's direction:

Tomatoes are red
Noses are blue
(In the winter)
Fly this person through time
To when everything is new!

As he said the last word of the spell, Sir Gadabout clapped his hands together, there was a blinding flash of light, and King Arthur had changed to . . . *nothing*! There was no King Arthur to be seen anywhere.

Sidney Smith looked at Sir Gadabout; Sir Gadabout looked at Herbert; and Herbert looked at the empty space where the King had stood.

"Well, I expect it's taking time to get his hair back to the way it was," Sir Gadabout ventured. "He'll be along in a minute. It *must* work – it's one of Merlin's own spells, and I read it *exactly* the way it's written in the book."

"Yes, you did, you bungling baloney-brain," said Sidney Smith as he pawed through Merlin's spell book. "But you read out the wrong spell. You *should* have used Spell 27 on page 74!"

"But it was the Time-altering Spell!" Sir Gadabout insisted.

"Yes, but that one was for sending people *forward* in time."

"Oo-eer . . ." said Sir Gadabout.

"I wonder which year the King is in now?" Herbert pondered.

Into the Future

King Arthur hadn't actually *gone* anywhere. He was still standing on exactly the same spot (with, unfortunately, exactly the same hair-do). The King was the same – but nothing else was. He had been sent time travelling, hundreds and hundreds of years into the future. To our time, in fact.

The most noticeably different thing as far as the King was concerned was that he was knee-deep in sand. If you've ever watched programmes where they dig up old bones and things from the past, they are always deep down in the ground. So the floor from the old days has sunk, or the world is growing bigger – I'm not sure which. But anyway, King Arthur was up to his knees in sand. And a small child was digging him up.

"What are you up to now, Effluvia?" the child's mother squawked. She was sitting on a beach towel and reading a paperback book called *Smouldering in the Night*. (Probably something to do with garden fires.)

"I've found a king!" the child replied, working busily with her little spade. "It's a real one, with a crown and everything."

"Oww!" yelled King Arthur as the girl dug round him. "That was my shin!"

"Doesn't look like a king – not with hair like that," remarked Effluvia's mum. "He's got a bit sticking up that looks like a pineapple with a parrot sitting on top!"

"I thought it looked like Winston Churchill sticking his tongue out," commented Effluvia's dad. He was sitting on the other side of the beach towel, reading a paperback book called *They Died With Their Hats On*.

King Arthur hastily tried to smooth down his hair.

"Never mind about his hair – he's a proper king and I've *always* wanted one."

"First I've heard of it," remarked her mum.

"But anyone would want a king! Can I keep it?" Effluvia begged.

"I should cocoa!" her dad replied. "You never looked after that rat you found. Your mum ended up feeding it, and it made a mess everywhere."

"*I* don't make a mess!" said King Arthur indignantly.

"Aww, *please* can I keep it? I could take it to Show-and-Tell at school."

"I would like to remind you that I am a Royal Personage," the King pointed out as majestically as possible under the circumstances.

"I can see that – I'm not stupid," answered Effluvia.

"Her education *is* important," said the girl's mother.

"Hmph," her father replied. "We didn't have all this education malarky when I was at school. But I suppose times have changed . . ."

"They certainly have," King Arthur agreed.

"Well," said Dad, "you can keep it as long as you take it for a walk every day – and don't let it sleep on your bed."

"*Yaay!*" whooped Effluvia.

5

A Knight of the Square Table

"There must be a spell for bringing people back from wherever you've sent them," said Sir Gadabout, furiously flipping through the pages of the red book.

"There are *thousands* of spells in there, you empty-headed noodle," Sidney Smith told him. "There isn't time to read all of them. We need to get him back *now* before something goes wrong with time itself."

"But if there isn't time to find a spell to bring him back, what the Dickens are we supposed to do?" asked Sir Gadabout.

"We've got to go after him!"

"Into the *future*?" gasped Herbert. "I'm not sure about that. It sounds dangerous. What if dragons have taken over the world and people are their slaves?"

"What if there's no Round Table?" added Sir Gadabout. "Or what if it's become *square*!"

"You could still sit at it, sire," Herbert pointed out.

"But I'm not a Knight of the Square Table. They might not *let* me sit at it."

"Enough of all that nonsense," said Sidney Smith, grabbing the spell book and turning to spell 74 on page 27 . . . I mean, spell 27 on page 74. "Playing with time is a very dangerous thing and we have to get King Arthur back in case he does something which will change the future."

"What if they don't have sweets, or lemonade?" trembled Herbert.

"Or chairs! *Then* I won't be able to sit at the Square Table because there'll be nothing to sit on!"

But Sidney Smith had already started chanting:

Tomatoes are red
Noses are blue
(In the winter)
Fly these people through time
To when everything is new!

"I don't want to stand at the Square Table!" wailed Sir Gadabout. "I don't want to go!"

And with that, he went!

6

To the Castle

King Arthur knew that something very strange had happened, but he wasn't sure what. He decided the best thing for the time being was to go along with what these peculiar people in their peculiar clothes said. At least he would have food and somewhere to live until he worked out what this place was that Sir Gadabout had sent him to.

Effluvia and her family packed their beach things and went to the car.

"Is this little box your house?" King Arthur asked the girl as they all got in.

"Don't be silly! Our house is much bigger than this."

King Arthur was relieved – until the car drove away. Effluvia's dad was a rather fast driver.

"*Aargh!*" screamed King Arthur. "The earth's moving! Earthquake!"

"Don't be silly – *we're* moving. This little box is called a 'car'."

"But it's faster than a horse!" said the King.

"I should say so!" said Effluvia's dad. "This is the double-injection turbo-spark-plug model. Now, I could have gone for the straight-back, high–intensity gizmo version, which in theory has more torque and lateral inflexion, but in my opinion . . ."

He went on like this for quite some time. King Arthur wasn't sure what language he had suddenly started speaking, but suspected it might have been German. And they weren't out of the car park yet.

Once they were, Effluvia's dad really put his foot down. King Arthur closed his eyes, held on tightly to his seat, and went very pale.

"Where are we going?" Effluvia asked after a few minutes.

"We're going to King Arthur's castle!" said Effluvia's mum.

"Marvellous!" exclaimed King Arthur, perking up and forgetting, for the time being, that the world was rushing by in a blur.

"Yes, you'll enjoy that, being a king and everything," Effluvia commented.

"Actually," smiled King Arthur, "I *am* King Arthur!"

"Yeah, right," said Effluvia. "And I'm the Queen of Sheba."

"Really?" King Arthur held out his hand. "I'm very pleased to meet you, Your Majesty."

"Where is this castle, anyway?" asked Effluvia.

"Well," said King Arthur, "you take the trail from the Great Pack Road, and at Mordin's Dyke you follow the edge of—"

"It's just off the A39," said Effluvia's dad.

"A place called Tintagel!" added Effluvia's mum.

"No, it's not!" said King Arthur. "Sir Ivor the Indisputable's castle is at Tintagel. Mine's *much* bigger, and a few miles down the road. In fact, if Tintagel is this way, my castle would be roughly where we've just come from . . . which is odd . . . "

"These kings," grumbled Effluvia's dad. "Always think they've got the biggest of everything."

7

The Future is Mobile

Sidney Smith's spell successfully transported himself, Sir Gadabout and Herbert to where King Arthur had arrived in the future – but there was now no sign of him. All they could see was a large, elaborate sandcastle with lots of towers and walls which Effluvia had made before discovering King Arthur.

"Oh, no!" cried Sir Gadabout when he saw it. "The spell hasn't worked. Look at Camelot – we've been turned into GIANTS instead!"

Herbert smiled dreamily. "I always wanted to be a bit bigger . . ."

"You pair of pea-brains! That's not a real castle, and look at those people lying on the sand over there." He pointed to a man and woman sunbathing on the sand. "They're the same size as us."

"We could ask them if they know where King Arthur is," suggested Herbert.

"But – but – they've got hardly any clothes on – just sort of brightly-coloured under-wear!" Sir Gadabout noted. "*Eek! People in the future don't wear clothes!*"

"Well, we don't want to scare them – you two had better take yours off too. *I'll* be all right, of course," chuckled Sidney Smith.

So Sir Gadabout took his armour and everything else off until he was down to his Baggy Breeches boxer shorts (a Christmas present from his Aunty Nellie) and Herbert stripped down to his Knightly Scenes Knickers, which had little pictures of jousting knights all over them (he picked them up in a sale at the Camelot Gift Shop).

Then, the three of them strolled as casually as possible over to the man and woman.

"*You'd better let me do the talking,*" whispered Sir Gadabout.

Sidney Smith put a despairing paw to his head.

"Good day, and excuse us," began Sir Gadabout. The two people sat up. "As you can see, we are just ordinary people of the future with no clothes on like your good selves, so there is no cause for alarm."

There was a cat-like groan.

The man and woman began to look a little nervous.

"We are looking for King Arthur, and we wondered if you might have seen him."

The man and woman looked even more nervous – in fact, positively alarmed, and Sidney Smith could stand it no longer. "You're scaring them, you babbling blunderbonce! Just leave everything to me and I'll soon—"

But before Sidney Smith could finish, the man and woman had already run halfway down the beach, screaming and shouting.

"Looks like there aren't any talking cats in the future either," Herbert said.

"Well, really. I thought *all* cats would be talking by now," said a disgusted Sidney Smith.

They wandered away from the beach, and soon Herbert spotted a brown direction sign by the road. "Look! It says *Tintagel – King Arthur's Castle*."

"But Tintagel is where Sir Ivor the Indisputable lives, not King Arthur."

"Perhaps they've got it a bit wrong over the years, but it's all we've got to go on. Let's head that way," said Sidney Smith.

"Follow me!" said Sir Gadabout, taking up the rear.

Along the way, they walked through a village. Here, things seemed quite different from the beach they had come from.

"Er, everyone's wearing clothes," Sir Gadabout noticed.

"Nothing we can do about that now – you left yours behind!" chortled Sidney Smith.

"And they all seem to be talking into little boxes as they walk along," said Herbert.

"How strange!" said Sir Gadabout. "But I suppose we'd better join in. Look – here's a shop that sells them. Wait here, men, and I'll get us one each."

A few minutes later, Sir Gadabout came out of the shop empty-handed and looking very dischuffed.

"They said I wasn't dressed properly and frightening an old lady. What's wrong with Baggy Breeches boxer shorts? Anyway, I don't trust them. The sign said their little boxes are all supposed to be orange – but *none* of them

were orange as far as I could see. There's only
one thing for it: find anything that looks like
one of those little boxes and just pretend!"

They looked all round the village. Herbert
found a large stone, Sidney Smith came
across an old juice carton, and Sir Gadabout,
who was beginning to run out of ideas,
could only come up with a traffic cone.

"Yo, dude!" said Sir Gadabout into his
traffic cone.

"Eh?" said Herbert into his stone.

"I've been listening to the things you are supposed to say into the boxes!"

"Never mind that," said Sidney Smith into his juice carton. "We've got to find King Arthur. This way!"

"I'm on my way home, love," said Sir Gadabout into his traffic cone. "What's for dinner?"

He thought he was blending in to the future quite well. In fact, he felt that people must think he was a very important person of the future – possibly a Knight of the Square Table, as they were all keeping well out of his way and not bothering him.

8

Tintagel

King Arthur, who still didn't realise he was in the future, was very puzzled when they arrived at Tintagel. Not only was Sir Ivor the Indisputable's castle empty and all but fallen down (it had been perfectly fine two days ago when he had last seen it) but Effluvia, her parents, and lots of other people were clambering all over it as if they were looking for something. Quite why people would want to go poking round a fallen-down castle was beyond him.

"I doubt whether you'll find any hidden treasure," King Arthur said helpfully. "The owner wasn't as rich as people thought." But everyone laughed at him, so he wandered away on his own to see if he could find the pair of pliers Guinevere had lent Sir Ivor ages ago and never got back.

After a time, he realised that someone was following him. He turned round to see two little old ladies.

"Excuse me," said one of them. "But, are you dressed up as King Arthur?"

King Arthur scratched his head. "Well, I'd hardly dress up as Guinevere, would I?"

"Tee-hee!" the first lady chuckled.

"What did he say, Enid?" said the second one.

"He said, 'I'd hardly dress as anyone else here, would I?'!"

The second old lady laughed.

"Are you one of these people who puts on clothes from the olden days and takes visitors on a tour of the castle?"

"No," said King Arthur.

"What did he say, Enid?" asked the second old lady.

"He said 'Yes.'"

"Ooh, lovely. And such a handsome young man, too!"

Somehow, King Arthur became lumbered with taking a tour of Sir Ivor the Indisputable's castle. He didn't mind too much. For one thing, the two old ladies were very nice, and for another he could still look for Guinevere's pliers while he was showing them round.

"And this was where they used to bake the bread and cakes," King Arthur explained as they went round.

"What did he say, Enid?"

"He says it was the toilet."

"How exciting!"

Before long other people tagged on, and there was quite a crowd following King Arthur around the castle. It was all going well (sort of), until they came across another group of people coming the other way.

"And this," said the leader of the other group, "was where King Arthur pulled the sword out of the stone." This man was also

dressed as King Arthur. (But not quite so realistically as the real one. Obviously.)

"Nonsense!" spluttered King Arthur. (The real one. From now on, I'd better call the other King Arthur "Derek". Mainly because that was his name.)

"Oh, really?" said Derek with a face like thunder. "And who in all the world and the hereafter might *you* be?"

"I am King Arthur, and I'm taking people on a tour of the castle!"

"Well," Derek growled, "the last time I checked, *I* was King Arthur, and *I* was leading the tour of the castle!" He stuck his chest out and planted his hands on his hips.

"What are they saying, Enid?" asked the second little old lady.

"Apparently, they've both got pet monkeys called Ralph."

"So *sweet*!"

But the row between the two King Arthurs grew and grew, and the tour parties from both sides joined in (except the little old ladies) shouting and waving their fists, until Derek lost his temper completely.

"Right, my lot – CHARGE!" He drew his little plastic sword and started running, with the angry mob behind him, towards King Arthur's tour party.

King Arthur felt he had little choice but to draw *his* sword. This was the real "sword in the stone" – Excalibur. It was about a metre long, sharper than a razor blade, and flashed and glinted as it came out of its scabbard. Suddenly, the mob that had been charging towards King Arthur was charging just as fast in the opposite direction.

It was shortly after that that the police arrived.

"But I was only looking for a pair of pliers—" King Arthur tried to explain.

"Yes, yes, sir. You can tell us all about it down at the station."

"What a marvellous show!" cried the first little old lady, applauding enthusiastically.

"We shall certainly come here again!" said the other.

The Chase is On!

"As far as I can make out, sarge, his name is Arthur King," said the policeman who had made the arrest. They were standing by a police van in the road next to the castle. "He's a tour guide with a scary hair-do who's been going round threatening people with a big sword."

"Tut, tut," said the sergeant, and he scribbled everything down in his little black note-book. "*. . . with a bit sticking up*," he mumbled to himself as he wrote, pausing to study King Arthur's head, "*like an acrobat bending over backwards . . .*"

"Actually, sarge, I thought it looked like a zebra playing a guitar."

King Arthur licked the palm of his hand and tried to smooth his hair down.

"You know, you might be right," agreed the sergeant. He crossed the last bit out and began again.

Just then, along came two people in underwear, and a cat: all trying very hard to act naturally. The taller man was talking into a traffic cone: "Cancel my 2.30 meeting and tell Gerry to leave the files on my desk." The smaller young man was talking into a stone: "Tell Gaz I'll meet him and Baz down at the arcade." And strangest of all, a ginger cat was talking to an old juice carton: "That fish you sent me last week was off. Don't let it happen again, or I'll get Merlin to turn you into a slug!"

"*Don't mention Merlin!*" whispered the taller man frantically. "*They'll think there's something odd about us!*"

The sergeant stopped scribbling and gawped. The policeman who had arrested

Arthur King – I mean, King Arthur – took off his glasses (I forgot to mention those) and gave them a good wipe. But the weird and wonderful scene before his eyes didn't look any different even after the spectacles were clean.

"A very good day to you," said Sir Gadabout, hitching up his Baggy Breeches boxer shorts so that he looked all neat and tidy. "You appear to be some sort of knights of the future, no doubt wondering what this strange man – *sorry, Your Majesty* – " Sir Gadabout couldn't help whispering to the king, "wondering what this strange man dressed as a person from the past is doing here."

The policemen didn't say anything, but simply continued to gawp with wide eyes. Sir Gadabout took this as a good sign and carried on.

"We are also knights of the future, like you. I personally sit at the Square Table, and we all have little boxes to speak into like everyone else. They're not orange – but then whose is these days?!"

He gave a little laugh, and was very pleased to hear the policemen laughing too. However, it seemed that people of the future laughed in an odd way: without smiling, and with very pale faces.

"Anyway," said Sir Gadabout, "we shall be quite happy to take this troublesome man – *I do apologise, Your Majesty* – off your hands, a long way away, and you'll never see him – or us – again and it will be all sorted out peacefully!"

The policemen glanced at each other and seemed extremely interested in this proposition. The sergeant started to say something, but his words were drowned out by the sound of broken-hearted crying.

"He's *my* king!" wailed Effluvia.

"He jolly well is!" barked her father. "I've said she can keep this here king – as long as she feeds it and looks after it properly – and keep it she jolly well will!"

"We might need back-up," Sir Gadabout called into his traffic cone.

The two policemen let out long sighs and sort of wilted like flowers without water.

Suddenly, Effluvia's father grabbed King

Arthur by the collar and dragged him towards their car, with the rest of the family following. The policemen began to chase him, but Sir Gadabout set off after them too. He dropped his traffic cone, and it kind of skittled the policemen over like pins in a bowling alley, and Sir Gadabout fell over the top of them. Herbert tried to catch the family, but it was too late. With a squeal of tyres, the car took off, and all that could be seen through the rear window was a perplexed King Arthur, and Effluvia sticking her tongue out.

10

Down on the Farm

Sir Gadabout, Herbert and Sidney Smith
managed to nip into the back of the police
van before it took off in pursuit of King
Arthur. They soon wished they hadn't. The
fastest vehicle they had previously been in
was a cart pulled by a horse.

"*We're all going to die!*" Sir Gadabout
screamed.

Herbert didn't actually scream any words,
but he was making just as much noise. His
mouth was wide open and he was making a
sound rather like the police siren. This was
because Sidney Smith had jumped against
his leg and was holding on with his claws for

dear life. Poor Herbert's eyes were watering like a leaking roof.

This noise in the back of the van was so bad that the police sergeant had his hands over his ears and was muttering, "*This is just a nightmare and I'll wake up in a minute. Tell me this isn't happening . . .*"

Effluvia's dad swerved and skidded along the country roads in his double-injection, turbo-sparkplug car. Soon, he managed to get out of sight of the police van and turn into a narrow farm track, where he was hidden from view by a tall hedge on either side.

"Now," said Effluvia's dad, "we just have to wait while they go speeding by!"

But King Arthur knew by now what a hooter was (Effluvia's dad tended to use it rather a lot). As the police van came up to the farm track, and sure enough didn't notice the hidden car and was driving by, King Arthur quickly leaned forward from the back and pressed hard on the hooter. The noise could be heard for miles around.

The police van skidded to a halt and reversed back to the farm track.

"Bad king!" cried Effluvia, slapping King Arthur's wrist. Her dad put his foot down, and the car began to hurtle along the bumpy, winding track. He was going too fast, and where the track had a sharp bend to the left, the car skidded straight on and into a duck pond, sending the ducks flapping and squawking in all directions. It came to a rest with the water halfway up the doors and beginning to trickle inside.

Effluvia turned to see the police van approaching. "My king!" she wailed, clutching King Arthur's sleeve.

"My car!" said her dad, looking at the steam coming out of the bonnet.

"They haven't caught us yet!" said Effluvia's mum. "Everybody out and run for it!"

They all scrambled out, with poor King Arthur being man-handled by all three of his captors. They ran through the farmyard, causing pandemonium amongst the geese and chickens. The farmer came to the door to see what all the commotion was about, then whipped out his mobile phone.

"Police? Yes, this is Mr Harris of Ash Tree Farm. There's a king and three other people running across my land being chased by two people in their underwear and a talking cat! Can you send someone quickly?"

Seconds later, the two policemen ran into view. "Blimey — that *was* quick — thank you very much!" said Farmer Harris into his phone.

Sir Gadabout spotted a horse. Being a knight, he was used to chasing the enemy on horseback, so he jumped up and shouted, "CHARGE!"

Unfortunately, this was a big old farm horse. It had never charged anywhere in its life, and it wasn't going to start now just because some weird man in boxer shorts was bouncing up and down and making a lot of noise.

Sir Gadabout was left behind on the stubborn old horse shouting, "CHARGE!"

while the chase continued without him. Then one of Farmer Harris's dogs saw Sidney Smith and went after him barking and snarling, and there was nothing for it but to scramble up the nearest tree.

This left only Herbert. Not being a very fast runner, and seeing he wasn't gaining on them, he despairingly threw his "mobile stone" at them (not something you should normally do, of course). It missed by miles. They were by now in a field next to the farmyard. And in the field was a bull. And the stone hit the bull on the head. And the bull,

already pretty annoyed by all these mad people running around his field, had had enough. He scraped a hoof on the ground, snorted through his nose — and began to charge.

Suddenly, the chase was reversed, and everyone was fleeing back the way they had come. Sir Gadabout on his big horse, and Sidney Smith up his tree, were safe enough.

As the chase went past them, Sir Gadabout said, "Now they've kidnapped a bull *and* a king! How many pets do they want?"

The dog had been frightened away by the bull, so Sidney Smith nipped back down to the ground and headed after everyone. "Quick, follow me!" he said to Sir Gadabout.

"I would – but this horse just won't budge!"

"I mean, GET DOWN and follow me, you clod-hopping clown!"

By the time they caught everyone up, all they could see was the police van with its doors tightly shut, and a very big and angry bull standing in front of it, waiting impatiently.

"*I want a bull!*" came Effluvia's voice from inside the van. "*They're* much *more exciting than boring old kings!*"

"*You can cocoa!*" her dad could be heard to reply.

Sidney Smith and Herbert stood well back.

"What are we going to do?" Herbert wondered. But the answer was under his arm. All this time, he had been lugging along the big red book of spells, and Sidney Smith grabbed it and began to search through the pages.

"Ah, here it is!" And he began to chant the words of a spell:

Eye of toad
Tail of newt
Frogspawn, tadpoles and slime
Send Sir Gadabout, Herbert, King Arthur and
  me
Back to our very own time!

With a waggle of his tail and a clap of his paws, there was a flash of light and a puff of smoke . . .

And Home Again

The bad news was that they had gone back to the time after King Arthur's haircut disaster. Sir Gadabout was keen to have another go, but King Arthur said he couldn't *possibly* put him to all that trouble . . .

And as it turned out, there was no need because they had arrived back in their own time a few days later than when they had set off. This meant that both Guinevere and Simeon Snippet had already arrived back from their trip and were able to sort out the king's hair between them – up to a point. There were certain areas of his head which only time could heal, but anyway they had brought him back a NASA baseball cap to wear in the meantime.

Sir Gadabout hunted round for a mobile phone shop, since he'd become quite fond of his traffic cone. But he couldn't find one, naturally enough, as they hadn't been invented yet. In fact, he couldn't find a shop of *any* kind, because they hadn't been invented yet, either. But it was still a pleasant stroll around the villages near Camelot. He chatted to people and couldn't help dropping a few hints about what the future held – the Knights of the Square Table, people wearing no clothes and talking into little boxes and so on.

The next day, there was a big party at Camelot to celebrate the return of Guinevere and Simeon Snippet, *and* King Arthur, Sir Gadabout, Herbert and Sidney Smith.

"Thanks for the baseball cap," King Arthur said to Guinevere. "And I've got a surprise present for you!"

"I love surprises!" the queen replied. "What is it?"

King Arthur reached into his pocket . . .
and pulled out her long-lost pliers! "A little
old lady called Enid found them in the ruins
of Sir Ivor the Indisputable's castle."

"But his castle isn't in ruins. I rode past in
on the way home."

"It's a long story, my dear . . ."

Sidney Smith was talking to Tibbles, the
cook's cat, while they lapped at saucers of
cream specially provided for them. "It's a

good job they had me along. I wouldn't say
I was *quite* as good as Merlin at magic yet,
but just watch this space . . ."

Herbert was with some of the other
squires. "I knew that it had to be a brilliant

throw to hit the bull on the head and make him chase them all back, but I did it! Almost a *bull's-eye*, you might say! And do you know what?" he added. They didn't. "When I first arrived in the future, I was just about the tallest man in the world! Even now, I'm taller than I look, you know."

Sir Gadabout was showing some of the knights his mobile phone. He had made it from a breakfast cereal packet and sticky tape. And he had painted it. *His* was going to be orange, even if no one else's was. "People of the future will talk to each other into them as they walk down the street," he explained. "You can say things like, 'Did you say you wanted me to get the large size washing-up powder, or the smaller one?' but a lot of the time you just say, 'Yes . . . mmm-hmm . . . yes . . . uhuh . . . yes . . .' for ages."

And even though everyone thought it might be a very useful device to have — in some way or another — they still agreed that Sir Gadabout was the Worst Knight in the World.